VANISH

STAY AWAKE...

Read
INSOMNIACS
1 ROAD KILL
2 FROZEN
3 TALK TO ME
4 TUNNEL
5 BUZZ
6 VANISH

S.R. Martin

INSOMNIACS

VANISH

SCHOLASTIC INC.
New York Toronto London Auckland Sydney
Mexico City New Delhi Hong Kong

ISBN 0-439-04426-X

Copyright © 1997 by S.R. Martin.

All rights reserved. Published by Scholastic Inc., 555 Broadway, New York, NY 10012, by arrangement with Scholastic Australia Pty Limited.

SCHOLASTIC and associated logos are trademarks and/or registered trademarks of Scholastic Inc.

12 11 10 9 8 7 6 5 4 3 2 1   9/9 0 1 2 3 4/0

Printed in the U.S.A.

First Scholastic printing, September 1999

1
THESE ARE THE FACTS

There are five of us in the group. The core group, I should say, because every now and then we get a wanna-be or two who hangs around, getting in our way, trying to be as cool as the originals. We're the originals, don't go making any mistakes about that. The one and only (or should that be "the ones and onlies"?). Anyway, we're it. Everyone wants to be part of our group; everyone who's anyone, that is. The guys at school

3

who don't want to just aren't worth thinking about.

We are: Gunna, Tez, Hulk, Duke, and, of course, me. I'm the one they call The Beast. Not because I'm all that beastly. I used to go out with a girl called Joanna, who was downright beautiful. Get it? Beauty and . . . We haven't gone out for ages now, but for some reason I'm still The Beast. I don't mind. It makes people think I'm scarier and cooler than I really am. The five of us have been friends since our kindergarten days, but we don't go around reminding people of that. It would make us all sound like wusses. Which we aren't.

The place we hang around at after school and on weekends, when we're not down at Sammy's Video Palace, is the dump. Yes, you heard right, the garbage dump. It's not as bad as you might think. Sure, it stinks, but then so does Mr. Crutching, our math teacher,

4

and we have to spend five days a week with him. Compared to an hour of math, a weekend at the dump is like visiting the perfume counter at Sears (not something I make a habit of doing, unless forced to by my mother or older sister, I hasten to add). Anyway, the dump's where we've built the dojo.

What the hell's a dojo? It's our place. Gang Headquarters, if we were a gang. The Clubroom, if we were a club. But we're not really anything, so we had to find a name that sounded sort of official but without making us sound like we belonged to the Boy Scouts. We got it out of a Chuck Norris movie. He kept going off to his dojo to find a balance between peace and kicking the crap out of people, and we all thought that sounded just right. When I looked it up in a dictionary, though, all it meant was "a room." I kind of like that. You know, "I'm going off to think in The Room" sort of stuff. I didn't tell the others, however, because you never know how they might react. Hulk especially. He can take offense at the smallest things. (Come to think of it, he always takes objection to small things; people smaller than himself, for instance.) And when Hulk takes offense at something, it's a good idea not to be in the same room. Preferably not even the same neighborhood.

The chair was an accident. I mean, we'd discussed getting something better than the few old rotting cushions that served as seating in the dojo, but we hadn't made any concerted effort to do anything about it. It was more like, "Jeez, I hate these stinking cushions we have to sit on all the time. It smells like I'm sitting on a dead cat." General murmur of agreement from everyone else in the dojo. "Let's get some chairs or something." Chorus of "Yeah, good idea," etc. Then we'd all go back to sitting on our stinking cats and talking about something else. We didn't exactly have purpose and direction. The problem was, no one was in charge. What we were was a conglomeration. It means a mass of different things put together — I got that out of a dictionary as well. We'd sort of pick a leader depending on the situation. Like, if we were about to be beaten senseless by a group of bigger kids, Hulk was in charge. If there was something mechanical to be done, Gunna took over. Duke was always in charge of helping everyone with their homework. And if there were girls to be approached, that was my area. It worked out pretty well. Tez was in charge of accumulation, which meant he spent a lot of time rummaging through the dump looking for stuff. This, naturally, meant Tez was the one to find the chair.

2 THE CHAIR

Duke and I were in the dojo going over the biology questions I was having trouble answering for class on Monday. Hulk was there as well, only he didn't care all that much about biology. He was standing in the corner, working out with a couple of dumbbells he'd constructed from sections of pipe and car engine parts. They were as heavy as hell, but Hulk used to lift them as easily as you or I could lift a dessert fork. When he did, the muscles on his arms and chest used to bulge out so far it looked like they were going to explode. He had ambitions of becoming an Olympic weight lifter. Unfortunately, he didn't know all that much about weight lifting, so all he ever did was work with the dumbbells on his arms and chest, ignoring the rest of his body. It made him all unbalanced. If he kept it up, the rest of us figured he'd end up looking more like Pamela Anderson on *Baywatch*.

The door of the dojo — this is actually a raggedy old canvas blind — was suddenly thrown open and Tez and Gunna came bounding in, bubbling over with excitement.

"You'll never guess what we've found!" Gunna shouted.

The sudden entrance caused Hulk to drop one of his dumbbells, which hit the ground with such force it trapped one of his steel-toed boots underneath it for a couple of seconds, causing him to hop around like he had one foot nailed to the floor.

"What do you mean, we found!" Tez snarled. "*I* found it. You just happened to be walking past when I did."

"Okay, okay," I snapped. "What's been found? We'll sort out who found it later."

At about this time, Hulk managed to free his trapped foot.

"Gunna," he said in his most menacing voice, "I'm going to snap you in half like a twig."

Gunna took one look at Hulk lurching toward him out of the shadows in the corner of the dojo and turned tail and ran.

"A chair," Tez shrieked, also turning tail at Hulk's approach. Tez knew that if Hulk couldn't get hold of Gunna, he'd grab the next best thing, so he decided his best ap-

13

proach was retreat. So the three of them went thundering out of the dojo into the dump, with Duke and me in hot pursuit.

Outside the midday sun was blazing down, making a heat haze over the mountains of stinking trash. Gunna and Tez were leaping over piles of green garbage bags and around discarded fridges and stoves like a couple of mountain goats, with Hulk crashing behind them like an enraged bear.

"It's over here," Tez was calling as he ran.

Duke and I followed at a leisurely pace, knowing full well that Gunna and Tez could outdistance Hulk for as long as they liked. Hulk may be strong, but he's no Carl Lewis. Eventually the three of them disappeared, but we were able to gauge where they were from the shouting.

After scaling a rather demanding mountain of garbage, Duke and I found ourselves confronted by a fairly amusing scene. The

14

various piles of trash had been pushed around by the city bulldozers in such a way that they had formed a sort of hidden valley. Now, generally the five of us know this dump pretty well, even though the city workers tend to move the ever-mounting piles of trash this way and that in an attempt to create some sort of order. The area we hung out in, however, was perhaps the oldest section of the dump, so no new garbage was placed here. Most of the foraging that Tez did was on the other side of the dump, where all the new stuff arrived. Because of this, we'd pretty well picked over this area and it was rare for us to ever discover anything new or interesting. This little valley, however, was new to us, and I was surprised that Tez hadn't discovered it much earlier. He, after all, knew the place better than any of us. It made me feel like we'd found one of those lost valleys that used to crop up all the time in

Hollywood movies from the fifties and sixties. I almost expected a dinosaur or long-lost tribe to suddenly make an appearance from behind a pile of discarded packing crates and rotten garden vegetables.

Instead, what Duke and I saw was Hulk charging down the side of the valley after the other two, bellowing at the top of his voice about how he was going to tear them into little pieces. Gunna and Tez, of course, were laughing their heads off, because they knew as well as Hulk did that he'd never catch them. It was all part of the game. Right at the bottom of the valley, completely free of any garbage, sat a huge brown armchair.

As we started to follow the others into the valley, Duke and I found ourselves stumbling quite a bit, which I found strange, and it wasn't until we'd joined the others at the bottom that I realized why. All the garbage was loose. Now, this may not sound odd to you, but then you probably don't spend a good part of your free time climbing around in garbage dumps. You see, trash tends to get compacted by the bulldozers so that it takes up as little space as possible. It's like those shells you find at the beach that have been broken down over a long period of time and then joined together by sand. Eventually, I guess, they become rock. And this is exactly what the trash in a dump is like, especially in the older sections. I soon forgot about this, though, when I started to get closer to the chair. It was downright magnificent.

Now, I have a built-in appreciation of furniture. It comes from having antique dealers as parents. The chair must have been built sometime in the fifties, I guessed, and was designed purely for comfort. It must have cost a bundle as well. It was rather low to the ground, with the actual seat lower at the back than the front, so when you sat in it you tended to slide right back into it. The entire thing was covered in brown leather, which had become polished to a high sheen on the inside by people's backsides for forty or so years. The arms were almost two feet thick, and when you sat in it the feeling was like being hugged by a well-dressed giant. There were many cracks and scratches in the leather, but overall it was in pretty good condition. There were also some rather strange parallel scratches on the actual seat of the chair and a few puncture marks that had probably been caused by its stint in the dump, but even so I was surprised to find it here. With a bit of work and loving care, my parents could have gone out and sold it for over a thousand dollars.

"Hey, check this out," I said to the others.

On the ends of both arms were odd, curled bits of chrome, which looked like decorative afterthoughts. When you pulled on them, however, they slid out of the arms to form beautiful chrome trays.

"These are for drinks and ashtrays," I said triumphantly, glad I could show off my usually useless knowledge of antiques. "You could sit in this thing forever if you wanted to, and just have people bring stuff to you. The owner was probably sitting here with a drink and a cigarette when he kicked the bucket."

"Oh, nice one, Beast," Tez replied. "Really makes me want to sit in it now. Just because you live in a house full of dead people's things doesn't mean you have to remind everyone of it."

We talked like that for half an hour or so, everyone taking turns at sitting in our latest acquisition. Then we spent a good hour trying to get the damn thing up out of the valley, slipping and sliding down the walls of loose trash. If it hadn't been for Hulk, we'd never have moved it. When we finally got the thing out, Duke and I had to take a break. We're probably the weakest of our little group, and the others tend to over-compensate for us. While Hulk, Gunna, and Tez staggered off with the chair, Duke and I sat at the edge of the valley getting our breath back.

"Strange about the garbage, isn't it?" I said when I could finally speak again.

"What do you mean?" Duke replied.

"Well, it's all loose. Sort of like it's been blown up out of the valley rather than pushed down like normal," I said, looking over at him. He gave me the strangest look.

"You come up with some really bizarre ideas, Beast." He shook his head and laughed. "It's physics. Everything here goes down. It doesn't come back up again. The bulldozers just didn't go across this section. It was formed by accident, that's all. What? You think the chair unburied itself?"

Then we both burst out laughing and headed back to the dojo.

3 THE DISAPPEARANCE OF HULK

Being so big, the chair ended up taking center stage in the dojo. In fact, it took up about a third of all available space, and we were forced to take out one wall and make a few hasty extensions in order to accommodate it and all the other junk that we considered to be indispensable. There was no discussion about leaving it outside or anything, however; it was just too magnificent to do without. And our dojo, to tell the truth, had always been a fairly flexible arrangement; we were always taking down or putting up the walls whenever it suited our purposes.

After we'd got it inside and extended a wall, we all took turns at sitting in it and ordering the others around. There was definitely something thronelike about it and, once you were seated, the desire to tell the others what to do was almost overwhelming. Funny thing was, when you weren't sitting in the chair, you were always quite happy to do whatever it was that the person sitting in it wanted you to do. It had a presence, perhaps because of its size, and it provided the sitter with a definite sense of authority. It didn't seem to bother anyone, though, and it became something of a game to run around like servants, getting drinks and snacks for whoever was "in charge" at any particular time. We all took turns in the chair, so no one missed out on being waited on, and before we knew it most of the afternoon had gone by. It was almost by accident that Gunna noticed that the light entering the dojo had changed to that thick orange glow that heralded sunset and we realized that we'd all probably be home late for dinner.

"Bring me my large dumbbell," Hulk bellowed from the chair. "I wish to exercise my quadriceps."

Tez took hold of the large weight from the corner of the dojo and handed it to Hulk, who proceeded to balance it between his feet and his shins and lift it up and down with his legs while holding on hard to the arms of the chair. You could see the massive muscles in his thighs bulging even larger with the effort. His face purpled slightly with the strain.

"This chair is going to be sensational to exercise in," he grunted as he lifted.

"The only thing that's going to be exercised is my ear if I don't get home for dinner," I laughed as I started out.

Gunna, Tez, and Duke came out with me, all promising to meet up again at the dojo after school tomorrow.

"I'm just going to finish off my set," Hulk called out as we started to clamber off across the piles of garbage. "Never half do a set of leg curls. It'll throw your whole exercise program out of whack."

"See ya tomorrow, Hulk," I shouted.

"See ya," he screamed back at us.

I was right about getting my ear exercised when I got home. The table was already set for dinner (a task usually reserved for my good self) and Mom was slamming pots around on the stove, which was never a good sign. Dad was at the table with his eyeglasses on and a tiny scalpel in his hand, picking bits of grime out of a set of antique Chinese salt and pepper shakers. Mom and I had found them at an estate sale about a year ago. They'd been owned by some old guy who'd lived in Asia when it was still considered part of something called the British Empire. When we found them they were black and revolting, but Mom thought they'd be sterling silver underneath, so we bought them for about five bucks. Dad had been cleaning them up ever since and, even though it was a slow process, the results were worth it. He had one of the shakers totally restored and it gleamed a brilliant silver. There was this great dragon on the main section of the pot, and its tail went all the way around and ended up back in its mouth. It had taken him most of a year to get that one clean and he still had the other shaker and a mustard pot to go, but he enjoyed things like that.

Personally, I couldn't imagine spending around three years cleaning up something that you'd only use to garnish your food with, but to each his or her own, I guess. But I didn't get a chance to talk to Dad about his work, because Mom was on me as swiftly and violently as that dragon on the pot could ever have been. Mom can sound like a chain saw when she's pissed at you, and that night she sounded like an entire logging camp. I hung my head and looked as guilty as I could about being late, but what I was really doing was thinking about the chair and all the fun we'd have with it after school the next day.

When I got to school however, the police were there. And they were there to see Gunna, Tez, Duke, and me. It seems that Hulk hadn't made it home the previous evening and a search was now under way. Naturally, we told them everything we could about the previous day and Tez took them out to the dojo so they could see where we'd last talked to Hulk, but no clue as to his whereabouts could be found. When Tez got back to school he said the police didn't seem to be all that concerned. They just figured Hulk had decided to disappear for a couple of days because of something that had happened at home, but we all knew that Hulk got on with his parents like a house on fire, so that didn't seem right to us. We decided to meet, as usual, at the dojo after school to see if we could sort something out ourselves.

It started raining in the afternoon, so by the time we made it to the dump everything was wet and grungy and stinking to high heaven. Normally we wouldn't hang around the dojo when it was like this because the smell seemed to stick to you more than normal in the rain, but we figured that what had happened to Hulk took precedence. Inside the dojo it was pitch-black because the day was so gray outside, so we had to light the battered old lantern that we'd salvaged about six months earlier. It gave off a weak, yellow glow, but it was enough to make the dojo habitable. The chair was sitting in the middle of the room just like we'd left it. The only thing that was odd was the fact that Hulk's dumbbell was sitting on the ground directly in front of it. The reason we found this strange was because Hulk had always been very particular about his weights and always stacked them very carefully in the corner of the room. If you touched them it was quite likely you could lose your life. Nothing else in the room seemed to be out of place.

"Why didn't he put his weights away?" Gunna asked as he tried to lift the dumbbell with one hand, failing miserably.

"If he ran off," I continued, "why didn't he

take them with him? Hulk loves his weights more than anything."

Then Gunna went to sit in the chair and noticed something else. "Hey, check this out. There are all these new scratches on the seat here. Looks like Hulk got pissed at it and decided to rip it up a little before he left."

We all gathered around for a look and, true enough, there were several long, deep scratches down the seat cushion.

"I wonder what's up with these?" I said out aloud, though I was only thinking to myself.

We bandied about a few theories as to why Hulk would just run off like that, especially without telling the rest of us, but none of the ideas really made sense. Tez figured that he may have gone and joined a traveling circus, but since none were in town at the time I thought that was pretty far-fetched. Then there was some discussion about him heading off to the Olympics, but we all knew he didn't have any money, so that was out as well. When we finally got around to talking about kidnapping and murder, it was starting to get very dark outside, so that subject got skipped over very quickly and everyone decided to head home.

As I turned off the lamp as we were leaving, I heard a sound like dry leather creaking and a cold shiver ran up and down my spine. I turned quickly, peering into the dark of the dojo, but all I could see was the bulk of the chair dominating the center of the room. There was no movement anywhere. "Hulk?" I whispered, but the only reply through the silence was the sound of the breeze moving in and out of the gaps in the dojo walls.

For some reason, the sight of the chair squatting there in the dark made me feel distinctly uncomfortable. Deep inside I felt there was more to those scratches on the seat than I understood, but what that was I had no idea.

"Ya comin', Beast?" Gunna called from outside, making me leap half out of my skin.

I hurried out into the twilight, glad to be back in the company of my friends.

All the way home in the growing darkness a thought kept niggling at the back of my mind, and it had something to do with the dojo. Something had changed in there, almost as if there were something hiding in one of the corners, something I couldn't see if I looked at it but would be there in the corner of my eyes; a shape or presence that was not quite visible but not quite out of sight, either.

4
TEZ GOES TOO

We were all pretty miserable for the rest of the week. No sign of Hulk was found anywhere. The police were now taking his disappearance a lot more seriously and Hulk's father and mother had started putting up posters of him around the neighborhood, asking anyone who saw him to call their number. They got a few calls, but they were all from morons trying to be funny. Things like that are about as funny as having a boil lanced on your butt.

Everyone in the group was pretty depressed about it all and we didn't go back to the dojo until around noon on Saturday, which was unusual for us as we tried to spend some time there virtually every day after school. And even when we finally did go, we didn't do all that much, just sat around muttering to one another and glancing guiltily at Hulk's weights in the corner. I don't think any of us had ever felt quite so useless in our lives. It wasn't so much that Hulk was the life and soul of our group, but he was still part of it, and the feeling was like we'd had an arm or a leg amputated; we kept expecting to have him burst into the dojo, swearing and sweating like he did, pushing someone out of the way and muttering something about trapezoids as he picked up his weights. There was an emptiness about everything.

I finally suggested that we go out and do a bit of foraging, which Gunna and Duke halfheartedly agreed to, but Tez just shrugged off the idea and said he wanted to stay in the dojo and think about what might have happened to Hulk.

"You never know what bright idea I might come up with. There might just be some simple explanation that hasn't occurred to anyone." He sort of curled up in the corner of the chair and stared moodily into the corner of the dojo.

We left him to it. There isn't any point in trying to get Tez to do something if he's not in the mood.

The three of us poked around a bit, but we weren't really into looking for anything; it was just an excuse to give us something to do instead of sitting around feeling miserable. If we'd really been serious about it we'd have headed off across the dump to where people dropped off all the new garbage. That's where all the treasures usually are.

We were only about fifty yards from the dojo, idly kicking stuff around, when we first heard the screaming. It was a really off sound, sort of high-pitched and inhuman, almost what you'd imagine an animal would sound like if it was caught in a trap and in the process of chewing its leg off to escape. If I ever had to define terror, it would be this sound. It was as if whatever was making it had lost all sense of reason and had just reverted to its most primitive state.

"That's Tez," Gunna said in a really quiet voice. He said it like he didn't want it to be true; because, to tell the truth, none of us really wanted to discover the source of that sound, and if it was Tez screaming we'd have to do something about it.

We looked at one another guiltily. Then, without anyone saying anything, we all took off at a run toward the dojo.

Bursting through the door, we encountered something so weird that it stopped us dead in our tracks. Tez was being swallowed by the chair.

All we could see of him was his head and shoulders. The rest of him seemed to have disappeared between the back and the seat cushion. He had a look of absolute terror on his face and was scrabbling madly at the seat with both hands, his mouth extended as far as it could go and that awful noise coming out of his throat.

Gunna, Duke, and I stood there with our mouths open.

"HELP!" Tez screamed, and right at that

moment the whole chair made a disgusting buckling movement, which looked a whole lot like a throat swallowing, and Tez slipped even farther down, his head disappearing altogether.

This sort of galvanized us into action, and I leaped forward and managed to grab one of his hands, bracing my knees against the arms of the chair to stop myself from following him. Duke and Gunna grabbed me by the waist.

From somewhere inside the chair I heard Tez's muffled voice screaming, "Don't let go! Don't let go!" And then the chair gave another immense swallow and I felt Tez's hand starting to slip from my grasp. I didn't want to let go, but if I kept holding on as tightly as I was I knew that I'd be following him into the chair. It was probably the hardest thing I've ever had to do, deciding to let go of my friend's hand, but there was nothing else I could do. As it was, I held on until my own hands were starting to slide in after him.

When I finally gave him up to the chair, Duke, Gunna, and I flew back across the dojo and ended up in an ungainly pile against the far wall, but were up on our feet again in a fraction of a second. We leaped across to the chair but there was no sign of Tez, just a few fresh scratches on the seat.

"So who's going to put their hand in to see if he's there?" Gunna whispered.

Neither Duke nor I replied.

One thing, though. We now all knew exactly what had happened to Hulk. We were just going to have a hell of a time trying to explain it to the police and his parents.

Each of us decided to try the explanation out on our own parents first and then meet back here the next day.

"No one sit on that damn chair, though," I whispered to the others as we left the dojo.

5 DECISIONS

I tried, but my parents laughed so much I thought they were both going to have heart attacks. So much for the truth winning out over all obstacles. Gunna and Duke had the same degree of success, the only difference being that Gunna's parents got upset that he could be so silly about his friend's disappearance and sent him to bed in disgrace. Duke's parents ignored him as usual.

Naturally the police started doing the

rounds about Tez early the next morning and we all told them what we could. We didn't have a lot of success there, either, though I have to admit that the officer who I talked to did start to look at me very suspiciously when I tried to explain about the chair. My mom laughed and said something about children's confused and vivid imaginations while she kicked me under the kitchen chair.

As soon as the officer had left I was sent to my room and told that I wouldn't be allowed out with my friends until all this silly disappearing stuff had been cleared up.

"You're all up to something," she said angrily. "I've talked to your friends' parents, my boy, and you're all telling these weird stories about chairs in garbage dumps and things that just don't make sense. None of you will be seeing one another except for school until whatever you're up to is solved. And that's that. Now you stay in here and think about that."

Naturally, I was out my bedroom window and down to the dump as soon as she closed the door. If no one was even going to try and believe me, then I was going to have to do something about it myself.

Duke and Gunna had pretty much the same story as mine, though neither of their parents had grounded them. The results were pretty much as we'd expected. We sat around the doorway of the dojo, unsure of how to proceed from this point on, each of us keeping a wary eye on the chair. It looked harmless enough, but none of us wanted to get any closer to it than we were.

"We've got to do something," Duke said, looking in my direction. "We can't just leave them in there."

"Maybe they're just underneath it somewhere," muttered Gunna. "You know, like in a hole underground or something."

Duke and I didn't even bother replying to

this. There was something about the chair that was way beyond our understanding, something other-dimensional about what had happened. Gunna crawled across the floor and peered carefully under the chair, making sure he didn't get his head too close.

"Nope," he said, backing quickly away, "can't see anything except dirt."

"We can't just leave them there," Duke repeated, looking even harder at me this time.

"Well, what do you want me to do about it?" I finally snapped back at him, knowing that he expected me to come up with an answer. For some reason it was always me who was expected to solve things in the group, a task I sometimes enjoyed. This time, though, I wasn't sure I was really qualified to come up with a solution.

"You're the one who let go of Tez," Gunna said sulkily.

"Oh, thanks very much. So now it's my

fault?" I must admit to feeling a little guilty about it, but I didn't expect the others to blame me. "It was you idiots who found the thing."

"Yeah, but we just thought it was a chair," Gunna replied.

"It *is* a stupid chair!" Duke suddenly shouted. "And arguing about whose fault all this is is not going to help Hulk or Tez. So both of you just shut up and go home or come up with some idea about how we're going to help them." He'd gone all red in the face and it almost looked like he was going to cry, which was not something Duke did lightly. "They're our friends in there. That *thing* has eaten our best friends and we're sitting around talking crap instead of trying to help them." He turned his back on us and sat staring at the wall. This time I was pretty sure he was crying.

Gunna and I looked at each other, feeling a little ashamed at our squabbling. Duke was right. We were the only people who could do anything at this stage. There certainly wasn't going to be any help coming from our parents or the police.

Guilt about letting go of Tez finally got the better of me. "Gunna, go grab that big coil of rope, will you?"

"What are you going to do?" he said.

"I'm going in."

Duke turned his red-rimmed eyes in my direction. "I knew you'd think of something."

I gave both of them my hardest stare. "Yeah. But you two are going to be tied to the other end."

Gunna swallowed very loudly. "This is going to be fun."

JOURNEY
IN THE DARK

I was sitting in the chair with a length of rope tied around my middle. Tied very tightly, I might add, making it a little difficult to breathe. The rope ran across the floor of the dojo and out through the door, where I could see Gunna and Duke tied to the other end, standing as far from the door as possible. We'd worked out that the chair didn't do anything when there were other people in the room; it had to have solitude for its work. I was moving around restlessly, feeling the sweat developing under my arms and across my top lip. To say I was nervous is an understatement.

"Anything?" Duke called out.

I was about to say "no" when I felt a subtle shift in the chair, almost as if its very texture had altered.

"Beast?" Duke called again, peering into the gloom of the dojo.

Then it happened.

All of a sudden, I felt the back of the chair and the seat behind me part and what felt like a huge, hideous leather tongue slide under my backside and catch the backs of my legs. They were pulled violently backward and I found myself facedown on the seat of the chair, the lower half of my body already swallowed and encased in a massive, pulsating throat of some kind.

I have to admit to screaming.

It's not that it hurt at all, it was just indescribably disgusting; and I knew with blinding clarity what an animal must feel like as it's eaten alive by something else.

Outside the dojo, Gunna's and Duke's faces scrunched up with terror, and I had the horrible feeling that they were going to untie themselves and make a run for it. That made me scream even louder, which only made them panic even more.

No matter my good intentions about my missing friends, my hands were scrabbling madly at the seat of the chair, trying everything possible to stop my backward movement. But it was undeniable. The huge constrictions of the leather throat that held me continued unabated.

My penultimate image of the world that I knew was of my two friends' faces, horribly contorted with terror, being dragged inevitably toward the door of the dojo. And the very last thing I saw, the thing that scared me more than anything, was of

Gunna pulling out his pocketknife and starting to hack at the rope that tied him.

I was encased in thick, soft leather cushions (that's what it felt like, anyway), which forced me backward in a ghastly gulping movement, further and further downward. My screaming had stopped by this time because I had no air to scream with. It was pitch-black and suffocating.

When I tried tugging on the rope a couple of times — the signal we'd prearranged for the others to pull me back up — it felt loose in my hands, as if it wasn't connected to anything anymore. There were tears running down my face and I could feel myself whimpering. I felt like calling out to my mom and dad but didn't have the air even for that.

This is it, I thought; you've really gone too far this time.

Which was when I hit bottom, both physically and mentally.

7 MIND SUCKING

Ever studied what a stomach does to food? I have. The acids start to break down whatever's in it, eating away until all that's left is the goop you crap out the next day. And I guess that's what started to happen to me, except it was working on my mind rather than my body.

It was like something cold immediately started to eat its way into my head, causing me to forget things, like who I was and why I was here. And it started the moment the swallowing motion stopped.

I was in a huge place, a cold place, and there was a wind blowing. And it was the wind that seemed to whip my thoughts away. Underneath my feet the ground was spongy, sort of like the seat of the chair; walking on it was difficult at first.

Shock is probably what I was experiencing, but the feeling was like when you suddenly wake up from a really deep sleep. I wasn't sure where I was or how I got here, even who I was for a few moments.

Then I heard the giggling.

It came from somewhere off to my left, sounding sinister and otherworldly, yet somehow slightly familiar.

I slapped my face. Hard. Then I slapped it again. I remembered my name and why I was here. Reaching out in front of me I felt the comforting presence of the rope. If you don't take a lot of care, I thought, you're going to forget why you're here.

For the moment, I didn't pull on the rope, not wanting to discover whether Gunna and Duke were still tied to the other end.

I felt someone run past me in the dark, which made me shudder uncontrollably; and the moment that happened my mind started to wander again. How long my mind drifted I have no idea, but I snapped back again when I heard the strangely familiar giggling.

"Hang on to yourself, Beast," I said out loud.

"Beast?" said a voice. Then there was another burst of giggling.

I started to crawl in its direction.

"Tez?" I shouted, which only inspired more giggling.

I crawled around on the spongy surface, this way and that, trying to find the source of the voice, and was about to give up when I rammed right into someone with my head. They gave an enormous whoop of terror and started to scramble off in the other direction, but I lunged after them, grabbing a foot.

"TEZ! TEZ! TEZ!" I screamed at the thrashing figure. It continued to struggle, so I dragged myself along its body until I found the head and started slapping away vigorously.

"Come out of it, Tez," I said when I finally stopped. "It's me, Beast."

There was a long, empty silence, during which I could feel the figure underneath me breathing. Then I had a sudden, very frightening thought.

"You are Tez, aren't you? Or Hulk?" I said, backing away a bit.

"Of course I'm Tez," came the furious reply. "Stop sitting on my stomach." Then his hands reached up and grabbed my shirt. "It really is you, isn't it? This is really happening?"

"Yes," I replied. "It's real, and I've got a rope. We're getting out of here."

"Thank God," he said, and I felt him relax under me.

"Don't relax," I snapped. "Focus on what we've got to do. If you don't, you'll forget and you'll be down here forever. Where's Hulk?"

"He was here, I think. I can't remember how long ago. He won't stay still, just keeps running around. How long have I been here?"

"Long enough," I replied grimly. "We've got to find him."

"I just want to go home," Tex whimpered.

"We will," I said as I hugged him around the shoulders. "Just stay focused and we'll get out of here."

Then I felt the rope go suddenly taut and myself begin to rise.

"NO!" I screamed. "Not yet, not yet."

But there was no stopping it. I reached over and grabbed Tez under the arms and hung on for dear life.

 CHAIR VOMIT

Gunna and Duke said we came out of the chair like vomit, in this huge gush of arms and legs and screaming and kicking. They said the chair made a sound like we'd stuck fingers down its throat.

There's only one thing I remember clearly about the trip back, and that happened just after the rope jerked us off our feet. I heard a really eerie sound, sort of like a wild dog baying in the distance. It was a sound full of fear and loneliness, a sound that I can only describe as madness in its purest form.

"That's Hulk," Tez whispered from next to my ear. "He's been making sounds like that ever since I arrived, but they keep getting farther and farther away."

"He's gone," I said, as I felt the rope tighten under my arms until it felt like it was strangling me.

It pulled us back into that horrid leather pulsing that felt like a throat, and everything from then on got scrambled up and crazy.

"Hulk's not coming back," I said when we finally picked ourselves up off the floor.

"Where's he gone, then?" Gunna asked.

"I don't know," Tez replied. "I'm just glad I haven't gone with him."

We smashed the chair into splinters with Hulk's weights. I guess you could call it poetic justice. As we were doing it I was surprised it didn't make any other sounds than those you'd expect from a chair that was being smashed to bits by four very angry boys.

In the end, all that was left was wood and leather and padding.

No one ever saw or heard from Hulk again, and we certainly didn't try and sort out the mystery for them.

We know what happened, but that's where it had to end.

As long as I live, though, I'll always remember the sound of Hulk baying in the distance, and I'll always wonder just where it was he went.

S.R. MARTIN

S.R. Martin was born and grew up in the beachside suburbs of Perth, Australia. A fascination with the ocean led to an early career in marine biology, but this was cut short when he decided the specimens he collected looked better under an orange-and-cognac sauce than they did under a microscope. After even quicker careers in banking, teaching, and journalism, a wanderlust led him through most of Australia's capital cities and then on to periods of time living in Hong Kong, Taiwan, South Korea, the United Kingdom, and the United States. Returning to Australia, he settled for Melbourne and a career as a freelance writer. In addition to the Insomniacs series, S.R. Martin is the author of *Swampland*, coming soon from Scholastic.